W9-AXY-281

Elephant Moon

Bijou Le Tord

A Doubleday Book for Young Readers

To Vérane

The author would like to thank Marjorie Kinder of *Animals*, the magazine of
the MSPCA in Boston, for allowing the quote reproduced here.

A Doubleday Book for Young Readers

Published by

Delacorte Press

Bantam Doubleday Dell Publishing Group, Inc.

1540 Broadway

New York, New York 10036

Doubleday and the portrayal of an anchor with a dolphin are trademarks of

Bantam Doubleday Dell Publishing Group, Inc.

Library of Congress Cataloging in Publication Data

Le Tord, Bijou.

Elephant moon / Bijou Le Tord.

p.   cm.

Summary: Describes how God created elephants to be strong

and powerful but also gentle and caring, especially in their relationships

with each other.

ISBN 0-385-30623-7

[1. Elephants—Fiction.]   I. Title.

PZ7.L568E1   1993   [E]—dc20   92-28234   CIP   AC

Manufactured in the United States of America

June 1993

10   9   8   7   6   5   4   3   2   1

The text of this book is set in 14-point Perpetua Bold

Typography by Lynn Braswell

BVG

Introduction

When I first thought about an elephant book I was aware that elephants in Africa were being killed for their ivory tusks at the alarming rate of two hundred each day.

As I learned more about these magnificent creatures I was touched and in awe of their intricate social structure. Elephants care for their sick and injured, nurse young females giving birth, and raise their babies with stubborn love. Astonishingly, elephants even bury and mourn their dead.

During dry seasons elephants dig wells in the sand for clean water, creating new water holes where other species come to drink. Always looking for food and fresh water, elephants migrate through brush and woodland, making roadways and changing the African landscape.

"It is from the group's matriarch that knowledge is passed from generation to generation — passing along where migration routes and riverbeds are and how to avoid threats, protect young," writes Marjorie Kinder of Animals, *the magazine of the MSPCA. Sadly, "It is the matriarchs and mature bulls that possess the largest tusks, the first target of poachers."*

Looking at hundreds of elephant photographs and peering into their eyes made me feel as if I were looking at someone I knew. Each elephant had its own personality, its own identity—and I thought: there is someone in there, inside that immense and beautiful wrinkled body.

Although the ivory trade has been temporarily halted, elephants remain on the endangered species list for the next two years.

Here are the names of organizations dedicated to saving the African elephants.

African Wildlife Foundation
1717 Massachusetts Avenue NW
Washington, DC 20036
1-800-344-TUSK
The AWF offers free fact sheets for
 kids about endangered wildlife.

Mr. J. Shoshani
Elephant Interest Group
106 East Hickory Grove Road
Bloomfield Hills, MI 48013

The African Fund for
 Endangered Wildlife
1512 Bolton Street
Baltimore, MD 21217

World Wildlife Fund
1250 24th Street NW
Washington, DC 20077-7792

New York Zoological Society
Zoological Park
Bronx, NY 10460
The Zoological Society also operates
 Wildlife Conservation
 International.

Wildlife Conservation International
P.O. Box 96984
Washington, DC 20077-7796

There
are
elephants
in Africa,
with beautiful
smooth
ivory
tusks.

There
are
hills and
great wide-open
spaces.
Plains
and
mountains
for them
to roam
freely.

There
are
trees, leaves, bark,
berries, nuts,
fruit and
grass
for their
food.

And
little
rains
and
heavy
rains,
to quench
their
thirst.

There
is fog,
mist and dawn,
with pink
clouds.

There
are blue
and
silvery lakes,
with
flamingos
and
white
egrets.
There
are beetles
and
butterflies.

There
are
elephants
in Africa,
tenderly
caring
for
each other.
Greeting
and touching,
reassuring
and
cuddling
their
newborns.

There
are
mother elephants,
gentle
and
tender.
Powerful
and
fierce.

There
are
little
calves,
playing and
trumpeting.
Cooling
themselves
in mud.
Splashing
dust
and
sand
on their
backs.

There
are night
birds
and
monkeys,
cooing
and
whistling.

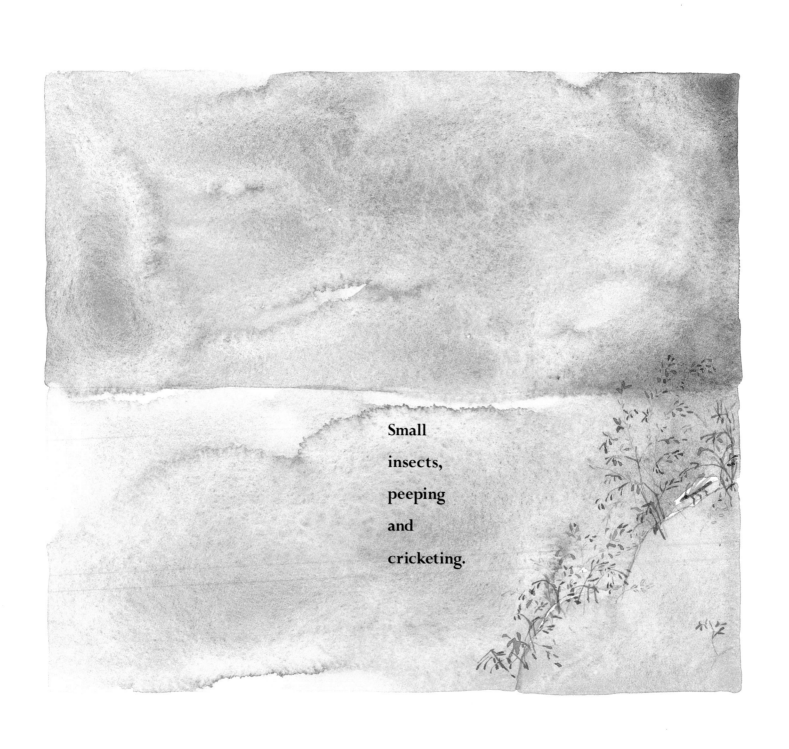

Small
insects,
peeping
and
cricketing.

There
are
elephants
in Africa,

peaceful

and

beautiful.

Sleeping,

in the

light

of the moon.